MORELIA

Juice

The Activist

A Picture-Feeling

Newcomer Can't Swim

To After That (Toaf)

Event Factory

The Ravickians

Ana Patova Crosses a Bridge

Calamities

Prose Architectures

Houses of Ravicka

Renee Gladman

MORELIA

a novel

SOLID OBJECTS

NEW YORK

Printed in the United States of America

Design by Erik Rieselbach

ISBN: 978-0-9862355-8-0

Library of Congress Control Number: 2018962141

SOLID OBJECTS
New York, NY

MORELIA

The sentence wasn't English but it was language none-theless. It used the Roman alphabet; it employed blank space to separate letters into various groups; and, most convincingly, the length of it ended with a period, that dot, that fleck of dust that ruins conversations. The strip of paper tucked inside the book I'm holding bore a declarative, which I couldn't read. I woke early this morning because I'd heard the door pull shut. It was an intruder. He should have left it open. The closing of the door concluded a dream I was having, the question of the dream: should I shoot this person? Yet the declarative was written in vain, or was delivered to the wrong person, or—in keeping with the novels of Lise Polak—was in reference to my dream, the very same dream in which I murdered a man in sunglasses.

It's morning. I wake with a foggy head. I stand up and stutter as if I've been drugged and watch the sun rise above the city. If I'm right about where I am, soon it will be time for breakfast. My body responds dramatically to the view outside the window—fear followed by surprise. I spit on the pane and then I laugh like a child, like snow and children. But the day's not right: it's the knocking inside me. It won't cease, no matter how much will I exert upon it. I've started checking the drawers to verify the extent of my hunger. They're empty. My bags are zipped and huddled together: I haven't unpacked. I'm new here. No wonder I don't know what to do. But the knocking goes on, so I must continue looking. There is a walk to the door that is long and bizarre in which nothing concrete happens.

A dream comes and covers. Will I tell him who's following him, who the people in the green sedan are, do I have the answer to Madame Mario's puzzle. And now he wants my shirt. I can't expose my breasts. He says, "I have something menacing in my pocket." What a poor detective. I tell him, "Your instruments are useless against me." His smirk falls to shock. "No," he says, "you're one of them?" "I am," I answer, though I don't know who *they* are.

I meet the side of the bed and fall over in alarm. It's the sentence again. I look at the first word, "Bze"; I try to think familiarly. I knew this word yesterday. I used it with a taxi driver, also in the lobby of a hotel. I had seen a man with a briefcase.

When I open the door there is no longer knocking. So, this is the source, or the real source has grown tired. In any case, I open the door. "The Mauritannica would like you to dine this morning, on itself of course," the uniformed man says. I let him in because it's true he has a tray. — "Nothing is wrong," he says. "You are sleepy. You are very relaxed. Your name is in our safe deposit box." "Is this marmalade," I ask him. I eat three pieces of toast, three eggs over hard, a deep-fried fish, a banana, and an avocado, despite a warning from my body. The "you are being poisoned" light is on. It doesn't influence me. I don't know why. The uniformed man waits at the threshold of the room. I can see the corridor behind him, the wall covered in tiny maps. He's moving his hips. I take my eyes away to guide the food into my mouth then return them to him. His hips are still, but he's brought a box to his lips. "Grun, grun, gern," he's saying. I look away, more food is coming. It's so delicious. I can't keep my mind off it. But I think I'd like to close the door. "Thank you," I say, "thank you and goodbye," and I wait. Does the light change? I move from the table to the bed. "You're a fuckster," I slur. "A big ass...." It's a different ceiling, I realize. Last night when I went to bed the ceiling had a chandelier; this one does not.

The dream stands in again. The green sedan—full of men—speeds down the crosstown avenue. Reforma falls from the street signs. I'm inside the car too. He likes the music, the driver, clearly, because he's restarted the album. We've been driving for a while. I know the time. I also know where we're going, but not well enough to pronounce it. A disturbance tears through the vehicle, as though something weightless is breaking, then, quite surprisingly, comes a voice. It goes on about Mr. Otis. How he ain't happy with me. How I left too much evidence behind. The man next to the driver is talking into a microphone. A thick window separates the front and back seats. I don't want to, but I say, "Talk to that idiot Granger," then something shoves through the air. "Get the Mickey," a man shouts, "she's trying to escape." Oh, I've opened the door! Some other is wedged between two bodies; I had thought it was I. But the air feels brisk against my face. And falling to the ground doesn't hurt as much as rolling and striking my head against an iron fixing, a pipe coming out of the gutter. The brakes of the green sedan sound off the way they do in the movies. I imagine the car beside the gutter where I landed. I imagine because I can't see. I can't see what's behind me. I can't see myself sleeping but I feel my breathing. I identify a certain sensation as my mouth. It's opening and asking where I am.

The sentence was in a new place, but it was still the sentence, same indecipherable words, same twitch in my brain ready to translate them. The first word I'd heard when I was on the phone with my brother, in the deep voice of a passerby. I was in the dim city. It was winter. So it would have been six months ago that I heard that word. Was that the first time? Nothing to verify the supposition. Best to leave it alone for now. The sentence, though, was not in the book I'd borrowed from a traveler at the bus terminal, which is a story all its own. And how amazing it was that I came upon that book; I had never seen it in that country before. I knew it because the title does not translate; it's the same in every language. The person reading the book was small and could be subdued easily. But it was Sunday, and just as probable that he would gift the book to me if I approached the exchange brightly. The whole thing took two minutes. When I placed the book in my bag, there was no scrap of paper tucked into the spine. Then, later, there was a scrap of paper. Now, there wasn't. The sentence, instead of being in the book, was taped to a window overlooking an enormous street. That's when it dawns on me: I am falling asleep in one place and waking up in another. My tongue is swollen, but neither my hands nor feet are tied. Nothing impedes my rising from the tangled sheets and walking fitfully to the window-pane, which is almost the height of a door, but isn't a door for it lacks a handle or any other instrument for turning. It has a sash, tied back, such that the city sits almost nude before me. Not entirely nude, because of the presence of the note. I reach for it; it's nothing new. It peels without complaint from the glass, even produces a sound. I look at the same familiar letters configured to nonsense and a light goes on. One of the words I've seen before. "Bze"—it was written on a poster for a rock concert given by a band whose name I have long since forgotten but whose music was ethereal. It must have been a year ago that I was in that place. The faces of the band members were not special, except that two were darker than the others, and you did not expect this where they were from, and nothing stood out about their bodies, except that written across one of them was that word—"Bze." The one bearing the mark was also the only one carrying an instrument, albeit only half of one. It was a violin bow. The violin itself must have been on the floor beyond the frame. But, even so, what was so "Bze" about these young people? And, more urgently, by what manner of transport did I arrive in this new room, where I've found time to lie down, where again I've come upon the sentence? The sentence is appealing, not only because it follows me from place to place but also because it seems to think about me. How can I jog your memory, it seems to ask. I try to take note of the particulars. Hotel rooms have a character about them that alerts one immediately as to where one is. This room is

8

no different. How strange, though, that I, or some power outside of me, keeps changing the place of my body, literally lifting it out of one bed and situating it in another, but never altering the nature of the place. What is different is that I don't have the hunger of yesterday—if in fact it was yesterday that I stuffed myself with eggs and fish—and today I want to go out. I open and close the door. I'd had a suspicion that someone would be waiting, but the corridor is empty. Another thing about the corridor is how green is its carpet and how I'm reminded of a forest. I must have traveled through one recently. My skin grows cold because the memory is painful. I am alone. There is a house on the other side of the forest to which I'm heading. Something will be wrong with it when I show up; somehow I know this. I don't want to go there, but it's something for Mr. Otis I've got to deliver. Or something I've got to do that is itself a delivery. I'll know when I get there. The pain is from the fact that I've lost some of my clothes and it's freezing under cover of the trees. I had to give up my leather jacket to escape the hole into which I'd sunk. My relations with Mr. Otis need to end. But it's one of those things where you can't say goodbye to a Mr. Otis. Somewhere along the way I pledged my service to him. As a consequence, he expects these outrageous things from me, like murder. This time I got caught and somebody's guard shot me. Thus, the ravine, the dirt in my eyes and mouth, and the loss of clothes.

I'm almost dressed to go outside. Wherever I go will be new, as this is my first time here. A funny looking city, with half-articulated bridges and water wells. I believe it's called Sespia. Everything in the room is branded "Hotel Saturn," and right below those words, every time, is "Sespia," which is a name I've seen before. I can picture it stamped onto a map tacked to a green stucco wall in a place that might be near here in which nothing happened. Because nothing was happening when I was in that place, I don't think I had much feeling when I saw the map. I wasn't looking for anything. It must have been in passing that I caught the name. I must have been going out the door as I am now. I must have been thinking something else, like how shoes are stacked. Yet I took a picture in my mind, and here it is today. This time I open the door to find a man standing there. I'm tired of this. He has a tray in his hands; I kick him in the balls. The tray crashes to the floor and the carpet beneath it catches fire. I shut the door. I open it. If the hotel is on fire then I must go out. Should I tell somebody? I knock on every door on my way to the elevator, but no one answers my calls. The man I kicked pretends to be unconscious, so I leave him there. Why didn't anyone answer? Perhaps they've all gone out for the day. When the elevator comes I hesitate—they don't advise riding it in an emergency, but that's ridiculous. I'm in a hurry. I reach the lobby and am stunned by the silence. It's not just the calm of midday. It's the dust and feeling of decrepitude about the place. There is no one here. This hotel is empty, a sign reports.

The sign talks about the absence of people, but also something else more subtle. This sign is taped to the window in the same manner as my enigmatic one upstairs. My indecipherable sentence that wasn't mine but wished to follow me. The sentence said something important; I am sure of that. Boris. Out of nowhere, the name pops into my mind, someone I haven't thought of in years. Didn't he have such a sentence written as an epigraph to that novel he was trying to publish? It began "Bze," and had seven other words like this one, though probably grouped somewhat differently, as I'm now recalling Boris' aversion to long words. He felt that people who employed them were aggrandizers. The sentence, in general, was an indulgence, according to Boris, who went away on a trip and never came back and never published his novel, at least not under the name Boris Borinsky.

If the place is on fire, I should probably go and retrieve the sentence, except that it appears to do fine without me. No, it's time to go out. Standing on the outside of the revolving door, I do the natural thing: I search for the farthest point on the horizon. In this case, it's a skyscraper with the letter

"M" on top. Around the building is sky, then about ten stories down are other buildings that appear newer in design. I look for a helicopter. I don't know why I do that. This city smells sad like pollution but is beautiful in how variously vertical it is. I have never seen so many heights. It's stunning, makes me think of dancing. I'm dancing just a little bit in front of this hotel. The door has stopped revolving. No one exits. I forgot to pull the alarm. How is the fire doing? And, no one tries to get in. I look around for signs that we are quarantined. Nothing apparent. Wait, why are my clothes so empty? I have nothing on me; I've forgotten everything. My passport, my portable honey. I don't have any cash or my address book. I have to go back. Oh, and I must make a sacrifice. I remove my shirt as I progress through the door and tear it in half. One half I place in the waistband of my pants for later; the other half I spit on seventy-three times. Standing in the lobby, I remove the string from my pajamas and use it to tie the ripped shirt around my nose and mouth. It wasn't planned but I take a moment to look down at my breasts. Don't I wear bras? They are so big. Who's my mother? Why can't I remember her name? Her face is clear in my mind, as well as the colloquialism "Mama," but what did our neighbors call her? I think these breasts are from my father. He was a glutton, like goldfish. But there's nothing I can do with them now, my breasts; I need my passport.

It's a slow-moving fire, I think. All fires the fire, also. Why does that sound so good to me? Who even knows what the words mean, not unlike my sentence: it's so sweet. I might as well grab it, too. But here's the thing—elevator or stairs? How much time has passed? Surely, my floor is already destroyed. But I've got to try, don't I? And elevators are for hurries. I call for it. The doors open immediately. This place *is* all for me, too bad it's burning. I arrive in seconds. As the doors open I adjust the cloth against my mouth. Okay, in and out, twenty seconds. Let's go. I rush out and a thug swings a two-by-four at my gut. It lands expertly. "All the while," I exclaim in response. He says, "Yit Ity," it sounds like. I'm furious. "Where's the fucking fire?" I assault his ears. He brings the violent wood up and slams it against my knee. "Where were you?" he shouts. "Frankincense, you motherfucks." "If you don't tell me, I'm going to knock you out." He's right in my face. His breath smells like cheesecake, I notice, as the day is ripped away from me. I withdraw like a weak fire, enemies all around.

Waking up is a question of right and wrong, but I don't know who's asking it, or where they have gone now that my eyes are open. It's a deliberate undertaking, transitioning from sleep to wakefulness; it takes me an hour. I've decided I won't rush anymore, regardless of what the signs say. In fact, I won't read the signs. I'll just paint over them. To be safe, I'll ask someone else to do it for me. Perhaps the woman sitting in the chair, who stares intensely at the bed. I'm not in the bed. No one is. Yet she goes on sitting there. It's a hospital or hotel room. I can't tell this morning, because obviously I've lost something. It's damaging. I want to ask her, but whenever I talk someone exacts violence. It's true that I've been using my angry voice. The shades are drawn. "Can I have some water?" I send off in her direction. "Can I have some juice? Is what we are related to what we have refused?" She doesn't respond because she's too busy thinking. "Hi. Can I have some water?" Beseeching her reminds me of my body. I need to look at it. I admit that I've already glimpsed my feet and been surprised by the shoes I'm wearing—first, that I'm wearing them, and second, that they boast an alligator print. I'm dressed quite spectacularly, as though I've risen in class. It gives me alarm. If I look at my legs and find that I'm wearing stockings, I'll have to change my name. Is it still in that safe deposit box? "Can I have some water?" She goes on with the empty bed. "Can I have some wine? I'm a bit parched," I say. "Can I have some water? Can I have some bread? Hello, can I have some water?" A few minutes go by. I move my hand. I'm surprised to see how far it reaches. It's not what I would call restraint. I begin, "On the count of three, everybody stand up. Everybody!" I yell at the woman, whose posture suggests she's not up to snuff. "One … two … three!"

Events roll. Two of them. They collide and make a loud noise. Something heavy falls past the window, drawing my attention to a piece of tape affixed to the glass. I can't ask about the sentence. It wasn't speaking to me. The woman in the chair murmurs as she stares straight ahead. It's just now occurred to me that she might be my prisoner, but I thought I was through with that. I had turned a corner. I can't make out what she's saying. It's on a loop, though. If I stay focused, I'll soon isolate the sounds into individual words. She's like my sentence, which I haven't seen this morning, my sentence, which all the time calls out from faraway places, even when it's right here, which it isn't today. That's weird. Don't I have a cousin called Bzey? Didn't she used to say, "You could get a 'Bze' and go somewhere nice?" I can't remember anymore. I'm too tired from getting hit over the head and shipped around the continent. The thought of a land mass brings on the effects of dreaming long before there are images, long before I'm off my feet. I walk around this room (alas, it is a hotel) and feel the sensation of my limbs becoming heavy with blood. I don't know where the extra volume is coming from, but all parts are inundated.

Despite the presence of the woman-statue (I've decided she's not living), I fall onto the bed, now under her gaze. I let the scene come because it's easier this way. No use writhing around, screaming *get out, get out*, when it's the mouth that conjures the dream in the first place. A man is talking to me like I've just walked into the room. But I feel as though I've been sitting here forever. "Can I have some water?" I'm surprised my thirst came with me. Is the sentence here as well? How do I ask him without raising his suspicions? "Is something incomprehensible lying around?" I ask with innocence. He gives me the water. "You're gonna have to start talking," he says. I thought I was talking. "We need answers." I need that ridiculous sentence. I miss it and think I might understand something about it now, like the meaning of the first word. But I need to see it next to the second one. There is a map somewhere, a map that vibrates when you rest your head against it. Some of the words in my sentence are calibrated to the vibrations such that when one pronounces them (were one able to) the map reveals its secret locations. I think. But I need lunch to prove my theory correct. "I am so tired of you," the man yells. He grabs my nose and squeezes it. "Ugh!" He jumps away from me. He hadn't anticipated my having schmutz in my pores, nor that my nose would suddenly look like cauliflower. "Use your hands," he screams at me. Again, I had assumed I hadn't the liberty of them. I remove the eruptions slowly. I need time to figure out how to set myself free. He stares at me with disgust. I chastise him: "It's your fault, Mister Ass. Now, where is it?" "Where is what?" "Something I need that doesn't have a name." "Mr. Otis wants your index finger or the truth about Simon Zuckersmit." "Smit, smit, why is that sound so familiar? The truth about Zuckersmit? Does he make maps?" And now he's got my shirt bunched in his fist. The dream is violent. I forget why I'm here. The people are short-tempered. I've found a way out. It's through his eyebrows. "We always find you," he shouts, as I burrow into his head. "See you again," I think he says. But I'm distracted by all the people here, this crowded city street, my book clutched in my hand. I've yet to read the new translation, being so busy. What I wouldn't do to find a quiet park.

A taxi pulls up to the curb. I jump in and begin, "Hotel—," because that's where I assume I'm going. Where else have I been in the last few days? But I don't know how to name it. They never say where I'll be beforehand. "Where are you going?" the driver asks. It's awkward. I expected him to know. Is my kidnapping over? I decline the ride and return to the sidewalk. I'm a pedestrian. It's not the city of my choice but a city all the same. I look around at the inhabitants to see how I should walk. Many of them have limps and uneven shoulders, but I don't get cocky, as they're both taller and thinner than I am. I want to find out the diet of these beleaguered people. But instead of grocers all I see are print shops. Naturally, I think about my sentence, whether I should have it printed on post-cards, to then distribute for a small sum of money. But I'm afraid to look inside the book for that slip of paper, for the possibility that it might not be there. And since I'm not in an enclosed space, I wouldn't know where to begin searching for it, were I to find it gone.

It seems that every major city has a capital building, and each of these buildings is ornamented in some amazing way. One finds the capital by moving toward downtown. The inhabitants here seem to be moving from the center toward the outskirts, which is not typical in this climate, which I think is morning. I've got to take steps in any direction before someone mean tries to clobber me. But the movement of these people is too choreographed. I'm worried I'm in a simulation. It would be sad not to be in reality. Talking to someone should resolve the issue. If the voice sounds tinny, then I've got a problem, not that being stuck in an unfriendly place (no one smiles here) isn't problem enough. But if I'm in some virtual space I won't bother with that walk to the city center. "Hello," I greet them. They stop and blink their eyes. No simulation would be this uneventful. Oh, and the city is eerie in its silence: the roads are beautiful, the tar freshly laid, yellow stripes newly painted, but there are no cars. The people emerging from the dense center are clogging up the road.

They're stiff but too well dressed to be zombies. However, they cluster like zombies, and the streets are empty of moving vehicles. Perhaps it's earlier than I thought, and I've just walked into the filming of a car commercial, this being its closed-circuit track. But why would the company use zombies to sell its cars? They are inhabitants dressed for work with no tolerance for language. Obviously, I'm afraid to step off the curb and progress through the scene. It doesn't feel natural. This would be easier were I in the city of my things. But I'm not. I'm in—I'm looking for placards. There are none here. "Hello." I'm trying a new technique. She stops and looks at me impatiently. She's wearing business attire and walking backwards like the others, but also has stopped here, which no one else has done. "Hello. Thank you. Where is everyone going?" I push my arm across my body to represent traveling. She gives me a "your arm's broken" look in return. I'm tired of talking. I reach for a place to sit down, which is a low wall directly behind me. I wonder if she will follow me in repose. She does. Sitting feels like a new recipe. But how much I'm talking! Though I'm not saying anything. Never this much in years. It exhausts me because I'm not getting anywhere, not in this city, not with these people. My wall companion pulls a clipboard out of her bag, looks at my forehead, writes something down, looks into my lap, writes more; she leans forward and seems to measure my girth, then draws several vertical lines. What's hardest about her change in behavior is that it compels me to talk more. I have to explain my stomach to her, but she has remained silent all this time, so I can't figure out her language, which one she speaks. I have tried several with no success. I keep looking at this place thinking it's Norway, this city being Oslo. But I get no response to my Hei. I say, "Hei Hei," just in case there's been a referendum. Still nothing. I'm tired of holding my stomach in, so I let it go. Full glory. The Norwegian laughs. I'm beside myself, it's the last thing I expected. Steam starts to rise from the ground as the air is depleted. Her laughter resounds through hallways. It's a tiny space again, a bathroom. I soak in a tub and stare at a city map tacked to a wall. I'm neither happy nor alone. The person here makes me more unhappy: it's Mr. Otis. "Who's the idiot now," he asks. I feel like since he's asking it must be he. My head is underwater. Now up. They need something from me. "Let me bathe," I scream. It hasn't been a good day. He's beside himself. He turns to his friends. "Goddamn it, I thought this was torture." "It is," they defend themselves, "It's the worst kind." I don't know what they're talking about but I'd love to add lavender to the bath. The room gets metal heavy. I think about the Norwegians. I emulate them, their reserve, their retro movement. I reach in my mind for a territory I can cross, though I still hear the men yelling. The walls of the tub become the walls of a room, where I wake alone. It's been a long time of the world like this, mean people, flight, and no food. But the bed holds me. I reach my arm out to switch off the light I don't remember turning on, and there it is: the sentence, in all its glorified foreignness.

Turning over is easy, but when I turn back I know something about the sentence that I had not previously known, and this surprises me so much that I reach my hand out to call someone. I have three of the digits dialed before I notice myself, my arm extended, the phone tucked between my head and shoulder, the arrogance of my index finger. Yet the automatic behavior disturbs me. Whom do I know? Whom do I *have* to call? Asking takes the pomp away. I forget what I'm doing. I have 976 and nothing further. I have 976 and the instinct to reach for a person out there, which is more than nothing, and it goes perfectly with what I have learned about the sentence.

The sentence just sits here now, so it's hard not to grow concerned about its authenticity. The same goes for me. I had been whirling around the planet, so fast that I was contaminating one place with debris from another, and all at once my travels stopped. I am sitting here. The sentence reaches out to me. I see it better than I ever have before. What I know about it happens two-thirds of the way through it, and it's an astonishing clue. It's almost a conversation, like I've asked a question and someone has provided an answer. If you don't know the language, your eye travels clumsily over the first six words, and if you're alert, which apparently I have not been, you reach something that is so familiar it makes you gasp. I put the scrap of paper down to smile: finally, after hours of wandering the streets, I have stumbled upon a door that in its grace reads, "Hello, come in." I'm talking about numbers followed by a comma followed by one of those illegible words. These are the components of an address: 874, stiasadern.

The problem of "in what city, what district" is a minor one. Just look at the sky today. It's covered in lace. Also, I've noticed something about the wallpaper in this room, which, at long last, is not on some anonymous floor of a hotel but rather is in a sunny room of a townhouse in a secret city, where I have stashed myself. I want the scratches and bruises I've incurred to fall back into my skin before I complete my original task, which was really just to go somewhere and read, to escape Mr. Otis and to read. The wallpaper repeats the map of a place, and I'm lucky in that it's somewhere I've already been. It starts with Sespia, the story tells me, the story that is not yet written. The sky has a look about it that says, "yee," like recycled toilet paper, like it's really tuned into the times. I think my happiness is climate controlled, and that's why I'm still undressed. Even though the room is artificially tempered, it's a climate all the same. I'm torn between the artificial indoors and the real out, as the two are approximately equal in temperature. Staying in will allow me to be myself, but going outside might lead to answers. I go out. I hesitate. I don't go, but soon I will. I have to make some decisions first: how will I introduce myself should I come upon a person, and, more crucially, how will I not get overwhelmed by all the numbers I'll see? I will want to go after every one of them, every house and store sign, which only will take me farther from the specific numbers I need to locate. I have to remember that mine are different from the others. I have two sets of three, in this order: 8-7-4 and 9-7-6. The first is attached to a place and the second to a person. I dress in linen and cotton to indicate that I'm free; I'm a person in the world. I gather my things—bag and gun—and as I near the door I see it: the book. Then I think something that does and does not belong: somehow in this life we have managed to fashion only an inside and an outside with nothing in between, and it's because we can't always pick the one or the other that we get lost and weary. I look at the book again and wonder if it could be our remedy, if I should go into *it* instead of out this door. Yet, having dressed so concisely for moving freely about the city, could I now, all of a sudden, switch to a burrowing-in persona, because that's what you need to "enter" a book. To get "in" you need to dig and get skinny and lose your voice; but you don't need to go outside, which is just the repetition of everything. The clock says *go*.

You go, but going is like staying where you are, just with your eyes facing downward and your body still. I went. I came back. It was reading. Yet it wasn't so much reading that I wanted to do. Or reading first, then something further, like walking. Could syntax become a city? It could, but I'd have to forget myself. I wanted to, but I couldn't due to the numbers and the undecipherable sentence and Sespia. Onward, I thought, standing on the transom of the door, the verge of the street. So there *is* only in and out. The news was discouraging. Yet I had to move. But at least I could stay fat and scream all I wanted, which now I was doing, but into the palm of my hand. Beneath the noise was the sentence.

Why was that first word so familiar? Was it the same "Bze" I came across in a medieval text on architecture I studied some summers ago in the soft city? A "Bze," which was a mechanism for counting time, something that would only ever be seen in the lower regions of a castle. To see a "Bze" you'd have to be a servant or a member of clergy— if my memories are intact. And didn't someone once grab the "Bze" from the wall and run across a field, soon to be gunned down, soon to spark a war?

The world had grown quiet. I felt my real journey could now begin. I could now head out into this city, which I had changed by first treating it as a book. I wasn't walking in the book anymore but I wasn't not-walking in it either. That is another thing that happens when one has read: the world changes. I stood on a street that flickered, in a mind flickering between scenes of attack and scenes of leisure, in a street that was both a dense street of traffic and one nested in a suburb. I preferred the urban one but felt I would be safer in the other. How did you walk as if you were in both? The sentence would lead me to Sespia if I allowed it to, if I let myself occupy the space farther along its length, where I'd discovered that address: 874, stiasadern. But I couldn't shake the strangeness of making the leap from "Bze" to 874, stiasadern, without reconciling that middle ground. It didn't seem possible that if one went directly from "Bze" to 874, stiasadern, that this would be the same experience as starting at "Bze," moving through a series of stations (still opaque but eventually readable?) and then arriving at 874, stiasadern. I was redrawing the map, and I didn't want to do that, because it would no longer be the map of Sespia. I would always be somewhere else. Yet this was a problem particular to the sentence. There was another problem that was the problem of city space, of physical environments. And I was only staring from the window.

The distance from the window to the street was an elaborate measure of the events of the book in my hand, the catastrophe of my recent experience, and this crossing of time and wood. I see faces in the floor, and sometimes they resemble Mr. Otis, sometimes his goons, but occasionally my own face and faces that were like drawings, sentences. Walk out the door, I commanded. Nothing will ever happen here.

To end the flickering I thought I needed to go out and commit an act in this new world, this city that I hoped was Sespia but was probably some city bordering Sespia or bordering a city bordering Sespia. What was paramount was that once I exited this door I would refuse myself entry to any others. I would stay out of doors and build my own interiors.

The street that opened the book I carried was narrow and lined with restaurants and shops; it was a nighttime scene that appeared to be carved out of a blur, out of a certain compulsion to become central to the problem of time. People stood everywhere in small groups and spoke and moved their mouths like French. It was a soundless world, but with conversations happening nonetheless. I knew this was the street of the book because of the number of times I'd read it, and it was always the same street, no matter the language in which I was reading it. The language of the book called into question the structure behind me, my safe house. On what threshold was I standing? Was it now the restaurant where Juan sits and drinks a bottle of Sylvaner and a fat man orders a bloody steak, which Juan experiences as an interruption, realigning the events of a story that has already occurred? It seemed more possible than ever to exist inside that story, though I had my own story that needed to be written, whose ending awaited me, and not too far from here, I suspected. Sespia would be the end of all things.

In my story, I was trying to be concurrent with the events that were happening to me, but since things had slowed I was less present. I looked out the door onto a street of houses irregularly arranged, perhaps to optimize exposure to the sun. There was grass and there was cement. And these were proportioned harmoniously. To activate the space, I would need to step out into the street and move toward the horizon, but which one—to my left or to my right—would have to be decided. I stepped across the threshold and turned right, for there was a sign in the distance. It probably wasn't for me, but facing a choice of sign or no sign, especially when you are in pursuit, you choose to go the way of information. Even if it's meaningless—you don't know one street from another—at the very least it provides a question: what's after "Stausensonnen"? I walked right, too, because there was the sun, which I hadn't felt on my skin in a long while. It wasn't like fire.

The sign read "S. Ausbinder," then it read "Boulevard," then nothing further. The rest would have to be gathered from the space around it. The pole to which it was attached, the lane of asphalt to which it referred. It was hard to walk without impediment. Was I supposed to just keep going? Shouldn't someone attack me, or the scene change violently? It had happened before that I believed myself to be safe when I most certainly wasn't, when, without warning, legs and arms were thrashing against me, and someone relieved me of my gun. S. Ausbinder was peculiar that way. Empty and ongoing like a vacuum. You could follow it to that fold in the sky. It was leading me to the center of the city, where, I thought, lay everything. But first I had to pass under this bridge, which, having appeared out of nowhere, seemed incongruous with being in a vacuum. I entered the darkness of the underpass and immediately met with discomfort. Some ironworks had been discarded in the middle of the road. It was like running into a wall. I gave out a cry, but it rose soundlessly. Even so, I waited for the echo. My sensors went out and came back with nothing, yet a much bigger nothing than the missing echo. It was a message about the silence of the whole, the space, the atmosphere, and not just that of my experience.

I picked myself up and exited the other side of the underpass. The works had exhausted me. I looked for a place to recline. There was nothing: no rock shelf, no streetside benches. S. Ausbinder was seeming less prosperous. In the midst of my search I realized that the book wasn't with me. I'd left it behind, at the place of my fall. The site of my injury was not the site it had been previously. A wind had come and changed it. Unsurprisingly, it carried a song (all winds do), but it wasn't the Beethoven I would have expected. It was more rowdy, like dance music, except there was no way I would dance, alone, at an underpass. I wanted to understand what it was about this structure—the bridge—that, combined with wind, produced this sound. I could tell the song was almost over. Standing there listening to it soothed the various pains in my body. I could go on now. When I reached down for the book, I heard "dahn dahn!" then nothing further from the song. It still may have been playing, but it had lost my attention entirely. Something tucked inside the book had yelled my name. It was a slip of paper on which was printed a series of words, interrupted by a three-digit number. As far as I could discern, it was a sentence, but not from any of the languages I knew. I stared at it, dumbfounded. What could it mean? I needed more light, plus I'd grown weary of the shadows beneath the bridge, where things appeared to be moving ever closer toward me. Back out into the open street, still no motorcars. I studied the book in my hands. It really was one of my two or three favorites. I'd read it passionately in every language I could find, even when that language was unknown to me. And how can I go on without saying this as well: there is this slip of paper that, for much of my time with it, has been tucked inside the selfsame book. My inability to read the book might have something to do with the illegible sentence into which I was, right now, leaning. It was not completely incomprehensible—there were those numbers and a word I'd seen before, "Bze." But when you placed something largely unknown into something remotely familiar, perhaps the end result was this.

It was an unstable city. Every city was. You were not supposed to just stand there. It would change on you, as suddenly this place had. The street sign still read S. Ausbinder, but it was really only that fact that had remained. How do I say this? The townhouses had multiplied and now were manifesting onto this side of the underpass. There were so many houses that the street had become a sliver. I could hardly progress. Actually I did not progress. I stopped. I held my hand up to block the glare from the sun. I shouted something unmemorable. Where was I going? I didn't want to think about the implications of the land changing; it would mean chaos for my itinerary. If this place were changing, would Sespia change as well? Was Sespia anything more than a question about communication? "Bze" came gently to me then, like a cousin promising something. Was Sespia at the other end of this boulevard that had lost most of its "boule"? I realized that if I went on standing there this would increase the probability that one of the occupants of these new houses would decide he was against me. I wanted to remember that it was the sun that had brought me here. It was true that being outside was just another kind of reading. You moved because the line was straight, because it had a pattern that called you forward. However, since the precise meaning of the sentence was inaccessible, so too was this city. I turned around to study the terrain behind me. I had advanced only a couple blocks past my hideout. There was no question as to whether I would return there. Reentry was impossible. But I did want to take in the short distance and compute it against where I was going to devise how long it would take to get there, with everything happening and slowing as it was.

A house was on my heels. I started to run—first backward to work up steam, then forward. But I had to run with my side pointing toward the horizon to navigate the slender road. It was barely a sidewalk now. I would follow this road until I reached Sespia. However, something odd was happening: I had begun to find that whenever I thought the word "Sespia," moments later would follow the word "Bze," but not happily so. These occurrences of "Bze" appeared oppositional to those of "Sespia," confounding my sense of where I needed to go.

To explore the relation, I tried to think "Bze" first. It turned out that I would have to stop walking to do this. Where "Sespia" was an idea you could consider while you were in motion, somehow "Bze" was not. But it was more than that I wanted to be able to think "Bze," I also wanted to learn something from it. That might have meant standing in place for a long time. Under an awning I thought "Bze" to see what I could learn from it. Nothing happened. I waited then I thought "Bze" again, more forcefully now, but with care so as not to induce a hypnotic state. This wouldn't be good. On the fourth go at "Bze," at the same time that I was growing sleepy, a field for thinking cleared in my mind. I held my breath, awaiting an answer. "Bze," I pushed out, deciding it would be my last. Something appeared way out on the field. It was so far away; it needed to come closer. "What are you doing here?" I asked, when I thought I'd made the figure out. But how could I be sure at this distance? I reached for it with the same part of my mind that wished me asleep. It came, but left me at once. And now I was under.

When I returned from my trance, I saw in my mind the monogram of Hotel Saturn. I don't know what had unearthed it but there it was before me. It said the same thing that I'd been saying all this time, but in a more startling way, because it was attached to something. I had been in Sespia before. How could this have happened? It must have meant nothing to me, my being there, because of how thoroughly I had erased it. This was an uncomfortable situation: now reenvisioning my journey not as a "setting out" but a "return."

I moved like I always did: covertly. That meant diving behind a sculpture when I saw my first person. S. Ausbinder had let out onto a square. It was vast and empty. I'd thought I was alone. I did my dance. I did it twice and was going for a third round when someone clapped and said the equivalent of "Hooray" in one of the Eastern languages. This is when I dove for cover behind a bronze man on a horse. I lay there, trying to control my breathing. It's a procedure we do: imagining a plain, picking up pinecones. I did everything right, yet I still heard her approach me, as if I were lying in the open, like this was a picnic we were having. She was commenting on my dance. It was all a jumble of flattery until— Did she say "Bze"? I lifted my head from the ground and opened my mouth to speak. I hesitated. It had been a long time. I wasn't sure I wanted it—human contact—after all those rooms and concrete. She opened her mouth, too. "Bze" was all around me, I thought between breaths. Also, I was talking, but it was useless. She was talking, too, acting explanatory, moving her hands around. We batted our eyes. The day was getting on. I couldn't understand a thing she said, except every so often what sounded like "Bze." But instead of beginning a thought as my "Bze" seemed to do, hers always came at the end. She spoke seamlessly, and it was only because she periodically gave a sharp nod of her head that I could guess where one thought ended and another began. Often she would say something something "Bze," then nod her head. Why didn't we understand each other? "I speak like you," I told her, "but I put my mystery word at the beginning." I shouted, "We have the same mystery word."

I didn't want to be in this plaza at nightfall. I remembered the book in my hand. Should I show her the sentence? Maybe I should read a little, tune her out, pretend she's a tree. "Bze," I thought to myself. "Bze." No clue followed but there was a new feeling. It was that "Bze" went with another word, which was not the word that followed it in the sentence. This was more like "Anhka." I tried the new word out on the woman. It made her stop talking. She said, "I have a gun." But was she threatening me or offering a service? "I have uh . . ." but did I want to tell her? "You have a what?" she inquired. What language were we speaking? "I have a . . ." then decided it was best to keep it to myself. "So small, so small," I murmured. I got away from her. It was like going in for dinner. "Someone's calling me," I said. She couldn't hear. It was no matter. She pushed the hip forward where purportedly there was this gun. People don't want to repeat themselves, but they want you to remember their threats. I didn't know the appropriate response. I stared at the exaggerated hip. You couldn't see the gun—there was no bulge, no holster—but perhaps every so often you smelled the gun's grease. It was about whether or not I felt the threat. She wants something from you, but she doesn't want to say the words. It's her problem, but it becomes yours when the two of you are just standing there. I thought "Bze" again, and again came "Anhka." I took a step to the right and two steps back and thought "Sespia" inadvertently, proving my point: you can't think "Bze" while in motion and vice versa about Sespia. And "Anhka," was it a place or a negation? She looked uncomfortable. It seemed to forewarn something. I think she was waiting for provocation. Wait! Didn't the tag on my shirt read "Bze"? I desperately wanted to look— I hadn't found a clue since "Anhka"—but if I grabbed my shirt to turn it around to verify what I'd seen, the woman would utilize her reflex response to shoot me. I needed her to go, and needed to be left behind, in this prime of my life. "Are you African-American?" she asked. I couldn't close my mouth. Where was I? "Is this Sespia?" I couldn't listen to her answer. It was too involved. With her arms, she cut semicircles in the air; the breeze picked up. When she'd built up enough momentum that I got that tousled feeling, she changed tactics. Hands held together, then pulled apart, then brought close again, producing a thunderous sound. Here, my reflexes kicked in, and I plugged each of my ears with a finger. This is when she said something. To be precise: something something "Bze."

Either I walked away or she walked away. I don't know now. Somehow, I think, we were both walking, as if in agreement: walking opposite paths. I remember swallowing a bug. My mouth had been open; I was yelling goodbye. Also, I was running, so perhaps it wasn't goodbye that

I'd yelled. It's possible I was yelling because I was afraid, or I was dodging bullets. Regardless, it was good to be on my own again: friends are not helpful. But it was getting dark out and nothing had happened. I hadn't gotten very far today. Night was approaching, and all I was was outside. The wind wasn't even blowing. It was like people didn't eat in my story. I wanted a fish fry but where was I going to get that? This was not a place, it was a question. The sentence said so. The sentence also said I should be in a vehicle rather than walking. It is difficult to explain how I knew this. "Anhka" could have many meanings and might have been talking to me. Yet this had no bearing on the fact that there was nothing happening in this city. I don't mean that there were no celebrations. I mean that there was no action of any kind, except for that which was now past: my encounter at the plaza. How could I find transport if there were not even the minimum number of people to produce a modicum of pollution? The woman and I were too far apart now to stir up any dust. Something sat warm against my skin. It was the sentence. I'd brought the book up to my face. I was hungry. This new feeling would change everything. I'd have to go this way instead of that.

I walked until I found a train. This might have taken years. But the train was there and it bore a name that meant a lot to me. The place wasn't one of my usuals but I knew something about it. You can't always remember why an experience stays with you. But, for some reason, you know exactly how to enter the station and where to find the lavatory. You've even managed to find a person to say hi to. My cousin approached me. I have rarely seen a person more pleased. He grabbed me in his arms and wouldn't let go. He kept saying, "It's done. It's done." I think he was my cousin. The train station had undergone a renovation, so it was more difficult to know people as you might have previously. I allowed myself to be swept into the waiting room on my cousin's shoulders. But I had to keep my eye on the arrival board. My train was due to arrive that day, though at what exact time it was impossible to determine. The information on the board was not like that of street signs, upon which the notice holds steady, simply does not move. In this case, each line on the board moved at a speed independent of the others, yet no line moved on its own. For one line to move they all had to move, and they did this chaotically. You got caught anticipating the arrival of the Eastliner train, because its line was one of the few whose speed didn't injure you. Unfortunately, this wasn't where I was going. Somebody might call it shuffling, but why move at such blinding speeds? There was the train I knew about and, somewhere beneath that, my train. All the while my cousin was going on about his new wife and how they lived in the country. "Where is she?" I wanted to know. This confused him. His wife's name was Lula, so I said, "Where is Lula?" for clarity. His eyes glazed over and a train pulled into the station. People started running all around. "Where is Lula?" I shouted. "Lula is my wife," he spat at me. He was angry. He wanted me off his shoulders. I wouldn't yield. I dug my heels into his chest. The station agent called out something over the P.A. system. It wasn't the name of my destination. My cousin was pinching me. It grew painful. I climbed down. I needed to go off by myself. I said, "Bye." I said, "Give Lula my love." I said, "Incidentally, do you know Sespia or another place 'Anhka'?" I said, "Well, it doesn't really matter." I walked away. He shouted my name. I looked back to see his face. He was standing with his arms stretched toward me. He didn't look like the same person, the one whom my mother called Fishu. His face had left the family, I was thinking. But it was my cousin: his arms were reaching for me. I decided to reach for him as well. We couldn't meet. I grew sad. We were brokenhearted. It was really the saddest day. Then I remembered my train. The place I was going was neither Sespia nor "Anhka," and that's why I didn't want to talk about it. Yet going there would address the problem of the sentence. No one told me this. It's just that ever since I saw the train station I knew what

I had to do. These words are a quote. The leader of my country said them. Even now this is he talking. Even now. I would board the train as soon as its arrival became clear to me. But where should I stand until this happened? And how would I know it was my train and not all these other ones heading in the wrong direction? I'd given up the board and decided just to ask someone. This station, which I had thought state-of-the-art, was seeming more and more provincial. There weren't any people to service you; they'd been replaced by water fountains. Everything was about staring perpetually at a shuffling board until you fell over with a headache, along with other maladies. I refused to travel under such circumstances, and said this to the water fountain in charge, getting no response, of course. I bent over to drink from it, to prove mind over matter, but was quickly admonished by a passing couple. The water tasted like grapefruit.

A train pulled into the station. Again, people began running around insanely, bumping into one another, rushing to be first in a line that they ran from moments later. So many lines forming and dissolving with no apparent purpose. Naturally, I started yelling in defense. I'd grown impatient. I didn't know if everyone needed to do this thing, if you boarded the trains this way. All the while, the schedule board was shuffling time like war. I had to depart; it was clear that I had no choice. I needed a fresh start, which did not exist for me in this country. It didn't exist in the country on our left border, nor the one south of us. I wouldn't be going north so its capacity for empathy made no difference. I realized that I hadn't considered the country to our right, across the sea. It was too late. I had something else in mind, which had more to do with the sentence than anything else I'd been able to think of. I just needed the actual train. Something came hurling toward me: it was a hawk. I asked somebody; she said, "Yes, it's a hawk." I took it as an opening to inquire about the other thing, the trains, how to find the right one. I asked. People turned to see who I was. That made me sleepy. I turned my back to them; something huge and dirty was coming. It held a coffee. Coffee, I thought. The person whom I'd asked for help approached me from behind. She placed a hand on my shoulder. She said things: they carried instructions plus other harmless materials. I knew, as I was listening, that I would follow some of them and disregard others. I had certain sympathies. Her hand passed through mine as she walked away and turned a corner. I felt strange, as if someone were watching me turn a corner of my own. But I hadn't moved. Nothing in me had changed. The station shook with the arrival of two or three trains at once. I ran toward the boarding area. Other travelers joined me; they seemed to think I knew where to go. A group of us arrived at a pair of escalators: Platform 2 was above us and Platform 4 was down below. I didn't know. I looked around. It was a matter of whom I wanted to follow. There was a woman and a man. A beautiful woman. A beautiful man. He was ascending, she was descending. It would not be possible to choose the man, I concluded. His feet were exposed; the toes looked too dry and fragile. I didn't think he should believe they were worthy of attention. "Excuse me," someone said, in a great hurry. I allowed her to pass. She took the ascending escalator. There was a certain kind of person doing that. The people going down were unsurpassed in their elegance; they didn't need to talk, they didn't shove. I made my decision then my body stalled. To proceed I needed to empty my pockets, say grace, look back over my left shoulder, think something I no longer recall before I could follow the conveyor down. The arms of the station folded upon releasing my train, as if to say no more passengers tonight, not one single more.

Somewhere in the city of my destination a light turns on in a second-floor window. A person, awakened due to grief in the lungs, stands in her kitchen. A light comes on, across the street, second-floor. It's late, there is no other source of illumination: the moon is dead, or hidden behind fog. The woman in her kitchen brings a glass of water to her mouth and waits for a figure to appear at the window. A light goes on, someone usually looks out but does not in this instance. Still there is the water in the glass. The woman drinks it then returns to nether parts of the house. Across the street, in a second-floor bedroom, a young person inadvertently solves a puzzle, first in a dream, then again in the moment after waking. A string of words that fits perfectly in this slot. He reaches his hand out to restore the room to darkness, hesitates at something, like, what does it all mean, and then completes the light-changing act. Now the street, now finally dark.

I wrote this story over ten years ago at the end of a strange trip, where a rat crawled over my back in my sleep, where I would always be between places. An excerpt was published as a Belladonna* chapbook in 2011. My thanks and love to that organization of warriors. And thanks and love to Erica Hunt and Dawn Lundy Martin for publishing a section of Morelia *in their recent anthology* Letters to the Future: Black Women / Radical Writing.

RENEE GLADMAN is a writer and artist preoccupied with lines, crossings, thresholds, and geographies as they emerge in the terrain between drawing and writing. She is the author of eleven published works, including a cycle of novels about the city-state Ravicka and its inhabitants, the Ravickians, as well as *Prose Architectures*, her first monograph of drawings (Wave Books, 2017). *One Long Black Sentence*, a series of white-ink architectures on black paper, and indexed by the poet Fred Moten, is forthcoming in 2019. She lives and makes work in New England with the poet-ceremonialist Danielle Vogel.